THE WOLF OF HEATHCLOVE MANOR

SADDLES & SCOUNDRELS NOVELLAS

CLARISSA KAE

CARPE VITAM
PRESS LLC

CHAPTER 1

*L*ady Josephine Darrow

No matter the weather, Josephine took the long way home, careful to give Heathclove Manor a wide berth. Snow, rain, sleet, wind, or even a warm, sunny day couldn't tempt Josi to cross the boundary between properties. The old Josi, the American Josi, would have bounded over and introduced herself to her neighbor a few times too many, chatting away like a young miss. But her brief marriage had chilled her once gregarious nature.

Her mare danced lightly around a puddle on the path, and Josi regathered her reins—a requirement on her spirited horse. The large paw prints on the ground continued to lead her farther from home.

She'd refused to walk near the manor in fear of Lord Fennyson being in the outer yard or on his beast of a stallion. Surrounded by horses and livestock since birth, Josi had never seen the likes of Lord Fennyson's horses. Each one was equal parts magnificent and enormous. Josi's father specialized in racing stock, long and lean like the mare she rode upon. She'd been tempted—many times over—to sneak inside his barn and have a generous look at his horses. But no one dared disturb the reclusive earl, not even Josi's late husband, who had a double serving of arrogance.

The earl was rumored to be a brute—worse than Sir John, her late husband. Whispers surrounded the lovely manor tucked beneath the hill below. Lord Fennyson was said to be a monster of men, large in build and dark in soul. His eyes were black as night and his tongue as wicked as the wolf preying on Josi's meager livestock.

Another pang of homesickness pricked her chest. She missed her father and the warmth of the summer sun on a California countryside. A lump formed in her throat. She missed the softness in her father's green eyes and the gentle comfort of his voice. Naïve, she'd not given thought to a good or bad marriage. She'd only known a loving home with acres of wonder and horses. Both her parents had been childhood friends. Josi's life had once been simple, easy.

When her Welsh pen pal arrived in California, Josi had dismissed her suspicions. Sir John had shown up on her doorstep with arms full heavy with charm and deception. And now she couldn't bear to tell her father of her misery in Wales. A fortnight. She'd only been married a simple fortnight when her husband drank himself into oblivion and took off on her spirited mare.

A howl ripped through the air. Josi's mare danced underneath her, a hoof pawing at the ground. There were only a handful of chickens left in their coop, the door having been pulled open by the wolves' determined paws. Josi was down to one pig. Her late husband had emptied her dowry the moment she crossed the Atlantic Ocean as his wife. Josi couldn't afford for the wolves to steal another morsel. She'd been tracking them up and around her house, but instead of leading her back to a den in the woods, their prints had crossed over into the earl's land.

She pulled her mare to a halt and released a long sigh. Yes, she needed to put a stop to the wolves' theft, but was an encounter with the earl worth learning where the wolves hid?

Lord Fennyson was nowhere in sight, and yet a chill ran up Josi's spine. Her housekeeper had painted a frightening picture of the man. His arms thick as branches and gaze cold like the wind from the north. Josi had known only two types of men, a deceitful husband with a sharp tongue and a gentle father with love in his eyes. The idea of another Welsh brute had her knees trembling.

Thunder clapped. Josi shivered. She'd been in this wet country for nearly six months, but neither Josi nor her horse were immune to the cold. Her mare whinnied, the call echoing in the dark afternoon. Josi wished for the hundredth time she'd not let her butler and other footmen go. Her housekeeper had begged Josi to write her father for resources, but pride had silenced her hand.

Lightning flashed across the sky. Her horse neighed, bolting underneath Josi. She grabbed a fistful of mane, her heart in her throat. Her mare devoured the ground, the muscled legs built were for speed not stability. One misstep on the uneven terrain could be disastrous but the steady rhythm of the gallop settled Josi's nerves. With one hand on the mane, Josi fumbled for the reins and slowed her horse to a gentle canter. The horse eased to a trot along the ridge dividing her home from the earl's.

Another bolt of lightning. The mare reared up, stirrups slipping. Josi swung off her saddle to safety.

"Whoa." The masculine voice came deep and commanding. An enormous horse slid to a stop in front of the mare, appearing as a wall of sheer strength.

Josi's mare spun around, its long legs shaking on the rugged ground. With a scowl, the man and stallion cut off the mare.

Once more, the man snapped, "Whoa."

"She's not a dog!" Josi shouted. Thunder clapped, swallowing her words. She wasn't a foolish woman, taking a green filly on a jaunt. Her horse was almost six and had been ridden nearly every day for four years. Her horse had generations of racing pedigree, bred for their speed, not bravery. Neither horse nor rider was used to the Welsh landscape. The mare would calm in a moment, and Josi would remount and walk home. She didn't need this man to intervene. Fear blossomed in her chest. She needed to leave before this Welshman unleashed his temper.

Lightning flashed, and shadows obscured the man's face. With long arms, he leaned over and snatched the reins of the mare. "Whoa."

Josi's horse danced as if the command had come from the lightning instead of a mere man. The muscles on its legs twitched, the mare's eyes flicking about with fear. With her palm, Josi petted the mare's neck, cooing softly. Her own pulse pounded. Josi whispered, praying the horse would calm to her name, "Freya … Freya … Freya—"

"Traveling alone?" The man dismounted but did not release her reins.

Josi bit back the retort. There was accusation in every word. His stallion hadn't flinched at the weather, nor did the beast care at all that another horse was terrified. This was a horse her father would ride. Fast horses had filled his coffers, but her father preferred a steady mount. He often teased Josi, likening her spirit to that of his mares.

The Welshman stepped closer. His hat hung low, covering most of his face aside from his chin. The left edge of his jaw appeared to be a different color, as if two different types of skin were sewn together. She could feel his gaze over her. Josi's face flushed, aware of her twice-patched riding habit and threadbare hem and the wild way of her hair. Embarrassment turned to frustration. She didn't need to explain her situation to this stranger.

"You." The same commanding voice returned. "You are traveling alone?"

"Yes." Josi reached for the reins. He lifted them above her head. Josi froze. Her late husband would taunt her, keeping his heart and any other desire she yearned for out of reach. "Give me the reins."

"I will accompany you to the stables." He didn't wait for an answer but began walking, a horse on either side of him.

"That is my horse." She ran in front him, and Freya eyed her. The poor horse was nervous enough.

"An American." The man halted abruptly. He was a giant of a man, his head well above Freya's withers. The width of his shoulders was frightening; his hands could deliver more damage than irate words.

Josi silently cursed the man and his hat. She'd love to level him with a glare but staring into a shadowy face gave her the chills, not strength. "Recently arrived, yes."

"The widow."

She cringed at *widow*. Josephine had helped train her father's horses from the time she was twelve. She'd accompanied dozens of horses to their future homes, her father trusting her alone to deliver the high-strung animals. She was more than the leftover spouse from an unfortunate marriage. "I am Lady Josephine Darrow, if you please."

"Darrow." The man spat the word.

She couldn't blame him. Josi had little warmth for her surname and even less affection for her late husband. She held out her hand. "I've raised Freya since she was a filly. I'm well aware of her spirited mind."

"You've taken a young horse out in the middle of a storm." His voice rose. He had to be the largest man she'd ever seen.

Tall for a woman, Josi had never felt smaller. She was on a ridge separating her home from the reclusive earl's under a darkening afternoon. She should be thanking the insolent man—not standing her ground and demanding the reins. There was strength in him, something that invited both her ire and awe.

Josi straightened her back and held out her hand once more. "I've spent my life on horseback. I'll not be tossed aside like a schoolgirl. There's a storm brewing, and I'd like to return to my home."

"Be on your way, then."

Be on my way? Her pulse raced, tying her tongue. Sir John would brush her off in the same way, dismiss her words.

The stranger turned and walked toward her home, a set of reins in each hand. Freya glanced back like a frightened kitten. The wind picked up, ushering a chilling breeze across her neck. A wolf howled in the distance. Josi shivered but refused to follow the wretched man. With as much defiance as she could muster, she shouted at the man's back, "Give me back my horse."

The man didn't slow his pace, nor did he spare her a glance. Groaning, Josi rushed after him, cursing silently in her mind.

"The wolves are leaving their dens earlier." He nodded toward her home. "They've been breeding."

"Breeding?" She coughed into her hand, a fierce blush heating her cheeks. She'd heard their cries to the sky, and spent her days searching for their den. She and her housekeeper double-checked the latches on the gates and tightened the fasteners on the doors and windows, not that the wolves paid any heed. The ravenous things had destroyed every coop and sty. "I can walk the last bit to my home."

"You might have spent your youth with horses, but when predators are in heat, they're irrational." His deep voice shuddered through her. He walked as if he was either stiff or hurt. She didn't dare ask about his health.

"And they are rational any other time of year?" Josi couldn't help it. This man was utterly mad. Before he could answer, she circled him and held out her hand for him to stop. "I appreciate your kindness but, truly, I can walk the rest of the way." She was already embarrassed. This stranger didn't need to see how desperate her situation had become. The sun dipped behind a cloud, shadows stretching long and the wind picking up. The trees bordering the edge of her property had already changed colors even though fall had yet to settle. Her mare danced next to the man while the wind chilled Josi's neck.

He nodded to the oak trees guarding the house and small stables. As if he was the lord and master of Josi's manor, he spoke low and firm. "Do not veer left or right. Get the horse into the barn and keep the latch secure. Run into the house, and do not open the door for anything, no matter what you hear."

Anger pulsed in her veins as the man offered the reins. She snatched them from his massive hands and marched home, her temper flaring with each step. A pang of homesickness pricked her heart. Her father had never spoken to her that way, nor would he allow his trainers to be brutes with the horses. Sir John was endearing only until he drained her dowry.

Josi had been determined to stay in Wales, her pride keeping her an ocean away from her loving family. Had her mother and father-in-law not taunted Josi, assuming she was a weak-willed miss, Josi might have been more tempted to leave. There was a feeling of leaving things undone if she left now. She'd given herself a year, although the wolves could alter her timeline.

A rustling sound came from her left where the gorse bushes gathered in tight bundles. The man's warning echoed in Josi's head. She purposely slowed her walk, her boots clomping on the ground. Josephine was *not* a sniveling schoolgirl. It would take more than a pompous man to make her knees tremble. But, oh, how she missed a simpler, kinder world. The wolves—she assumed—snuck near the house by the light of the moon. She'd not seen a single animal come during the daylight hours. She was safe for a few hours yet—the man was just trying to scare her.

The glow of the stable light sent a wave of relief through her, not that she'd admit it. Josi didn't glance over her shoulder. She hoped the stranger was well and gone.

The rhythm of brushing her horse and putting away her tack settled her. She rushed from the stables to her home just as rain spilled from the pregnant clouds. A bolt of lightning lit the sky, revealing the dark figure of a man on a horse. The stranger had stood watch while Josi had entered her home. In the shadow of her living room, she watched the man guide his horse toward the earl's massive estate. *Lord Fennyson.* Josi covered her mouth and cowered behind the curtain. The stranger, the brute with the stallion, was the earl. She should have known. She sank back to the sofa, her cheeks flushing once more. The true danger wasn't the wolves lurking in the shadows but the earl at Heathclove Manor.

CHAPTER 2

$\mathcal{C}$yril Heathclove, Lord Fennyson

Perched on the ridge dividing his land from the wretched widow's, Cyril cast a severe scowl. His leg ached, bleeding something fierce. A branch had torn through his trousers, slicing into his skin. The wound was bleeding like a paper cut, dramatic and overwrought for such an insignificant injury. He'd need to sneak past his butler before the fool could call a physician.

Cyril had been on his way home, his stallion steady and sure, when Lady Darrow had foolishly taken her mare out for a ride in stormy weather. The *argylwyddes* hadn't even bothered with a side saddle. Lady Darrow was just as arrogant as her late husband, Sir John. Like the rest of the villagers, she'd tried to peek at his face. He waited for the little minx to slip from the simple barn toward her home before urging his stallion forward.

His groomsman ran to him just as the rain came in a heavy gust. "I've got Atlas, my lord."

Cyril didn't argue but dismounted with a wince. He patted Atlas' muscled neck and limped toward the house. Slowly, he made his way up the stairs, nodding to his housekeeper. She eyed him, but he continued down the hall. Blessedly, he made it to his room without another servant seeing him.

A knock sounded on his door. "Lord Fennyson," his butler said.

"Not now, Brenner."

"You're a creature of habit, my lord. The physician is downstairs."

"Ratbag," Cyril cursed under his breath. He'd been quiet. His blasted butler had a way of knowing the injury. "I do not need a butcher."

"He's willing to attend to you in your room or downstairs." Brenner opened the door, his eyes downcast like a proper butler. It was all for show. He'd been privy to Cyril's childhood antics. Cyril had been the cause of many of Brenner's gray—now white—hairs on his head. "Which would you prefer?"

"You're a vazey—"

"I'll let him know." Brenner pursed his lips and furrowed his brow. Like a disappointed parent—instead of a paid servant—he turned his head and left.

Huffing, Cyril limped to the corridor. Brenner had already begun descending the stairs. Leaning over the stair rail, Cyril shouted, "I don't need a blasted butcher."

His butler didn't flinch. Nor did he pause in his steps. At least the widow had the decency to wince when Cyril spoke. Brenner did nothing.

Cyril mumbled another curse and glared at his butler's back. The damnable man had done the unthinkable and called upon a doctor. Had the butler not been triple Cyril's age, he would have sacked the old man on the spot.

He banged a fist on the staircase. "I'll not be sewn by a foozler."

Nothing. His housekeeper didn't gasp. Nor did any other servant stumble or blush at his cursing. He stomped down the stairs, wincing with each step.

"Lord Fennyson." Brenner stood outside his study, a wide Cheshire grin firmly in place. His gangly frame made his smile all the more ridiculous.

"I can stitch myself." Cyril had done enough stitching on the horses and other animals filling his stables. He'd not called on a doctor in years. Cyril would not engage in small talk. Or any talk, for that matter.

He marched into his study but was silenced with one look at the hunched frame. He'd recognize his childhood physician anywhere. His pulse slowed and frustration fell to the floor. "Mr. Thatcher."

The old man grinned, his face a mess of wrinkled joy. "I hadn't meant to disturb you, Lord Fennyson, but I'd heard about your mother and wanted to pay my respects."

"Thank you. She's been gone nearly two years." A lump formed in Cyril's throat. Memories of the old man's kindness flooded his mind. Childhood adventures filled his frame, reminding Cyril of a simpler time, a happier life. Of all the doctors Cyril had been forced to endure, Thatcher was his favorite—though the thought made him grimace. *Blast.* He hated the entire profession.

"I heard you've got an injury. Might I have a look?" Heavy with age, Mr. Thatcher's voice shook.

A few minutes later, Mr. Thatcher reminisced about their shared history and the other patients he'd cared for, a vain effort to calm Cyril's mind as the old man stitched his leg. No other physician could still the hammering of Cyril's heart.

Cyril had vowed to never let another doctor touch him. He was twelve when the first white patch appeared on his hands. Within weeks the pale skin had taken over his arms and face. His mother was as pretty as she was dimwitted, dragging him all over England and the continent in search of a cure. Some physicians deemed him dangerous, calling his condition *white leprosy.* Others boldly stated he had leucoderma. The more absurd believed Cyril was possessed. One idiotic butcher had diced parts of his neck and stitched the patches to his face. He'd once looked like his parents; now he resembled a quilt.

Stitch by stitch, Thatcher took an eternity to sew Cyril's skin back together. Cyril caught Brenner's gaze. Pity crossed the butler's features.

With the same gentle care he'd always shown, Mr. Thatcher tied the last stitch and packed up his small medical bag. He placed a trembling hand on Cyril's shoulder and smiled softly. "'Tis a pleasure, Lord Fennyson. You were always a favorite." He winked at Brenner, adding, "And you're still just as mischievous as ever."

Brenner placed his hands together in mock prayer. "I have been sainted for my service here."

Chuckling softly, Mr. Thatcher shuffled next to Brenner, toward the door. They were only a decade apart, but both men had helped shaped Cyril, stood by him when Cyril's father had abandoned the misshapen son.

"Tomorrow." Brenner appeared in the doorframe, his lanky figure like an oversized cane. "You can give me the boot tomorrow."

Cyril swallowed the rising emotion. Both Brenner and Mr. Thatcher had always been kind, like his mother. A blanket of warm memories had not yet slipped from his mind. "How long have you known Thatcher was in town?"

"When he knocked on the door." Brenner waited a beat before adding, "Is it time yet, Lord Fennyson?"

Cyril didn't bother answering. He was uninterested in being scolded, especially by a butler too bold for his own good. He only wanted to sit in the moment. Cyril was well aware of how foolish his attitude was toward doctors, but it took him a minute to recover, regardless of the physician.

Brenner cleared his throat and tucked his hands behind his back. If he donned a cassock, he'd appear the solemn clergy instead of the ancient butler he truly was. "Time to put the foolish games of our youth to rest."

"Youth?" Cyril scoffed and winced at his tone. If he would have been home earlier, he'd not have run into the helpless Lady Darrow. The warmth he'd felt went cold. Because of the widow, Cyril had missed precious moments with the kindest of men. He'd have preferred to converse with Thatcher instead of being stitched by him. "You speak as if you know what youth is."

"Can we skip ahead yet?" Brenner waved his hand in a circle. He pursed his lips. His gray hair had succumbed to white when Cyril was but a boy. "Can we run past your cursing and tantrums to the part where you admit your time would be better spent elsewhere?"

"You're insufferable." Cyril had made his mission quite clear. He would rid his property—and that of his neighbors—of any dangers, including the wolves. The villagers hated him. He'd heard the whispers. But pride was something Cyril had in spades.

"Yes." Brenner nodded and paced. "Moving along to the part where you...?"

"Nothing." Cyril's mood was as dark as the sky. He'd been so close to finding the den. The yawn of a tired dog echoed down the hall. Cyril had purposely left his shepherd home. He didn't need her running off with the wolves. She entered the study, her body lean and tall. She was half wolf, half Malinois shepherd. Like Cyril, she was enormous, but unlike her master, she was quick and graceful on her feet. Instead of greeting the earl, she went to Brenner, nuzzling his palm.

"Traitor." Cyril narrowed his gaze at his dog. He'd loved the rare mark—a star on the shepherd's forehead.

Brenner dropped his frown and broke into a smile. His face became younger, reminding Cyril of earlier years. A happier time, for all involved. In truth, Brenner had done more parenting than Cyril's own father. Disgusted by Cyril's face, the marquess had packed his bags and left, leaving excuses and a wife's broken heart in the wake. "She has excellent taste in people."

"Present company excluded." Cyril stretched out his leg, wincing as the stitches caught. He hadn't needed the doctor but couldn't refuse the gentle soul. Cyril knew damn well how to thread a needle. He and Brenner had worked side by side in stitching up the horses in his stables. If Cyril called on a veterinarian for every injury, the man would reside permanently at Heathclove Manor.

Brenner poured a glass of whiskey and handed it to Cyril. "I do believe Thatcher would want you to rest."

Cyril grunted in response. Both men knew Cyril wouldn't touch the amber liquid. The same blood of his father coursed through Cyril's veins. He vowed to never become the angry monster he'd witnessed as a young man.

"It is good to be reminded that not every physician is a butcher," Brenner added quietly.

The silence stretched between them. Cyril's frustration dwindled as the guilt crept in. No one knew Cyril's history with doctors like Brenner. Just the thought of another needle touching his skin sent a shiver up Cyril's spine.

Brenner placed a calling card on the end table, tucking the paper under Cyril's hand. "I found this in your room. The Darrow housekeeper came knocking again."

Grunting, Cyril flicked the paper to the floor. The widow neighboring his land was a relentless fool. The *argylwyddes* should not have been riding in the horrendous weather, especially with such a high-strung creature. No one with a sound mind would become a Darrow. Every member was a hornswoggle. Every word was a lie, and every act dripped with deceit. Sir John—Cyril sniffed—the *sir* wasn't deserved.

Brenner frowned and lifted his chin. "One of these days you'll be—"

"Stuck with my face frozen in scorn," Cyril finished for him. "That's not any truer now than when I was a child."

"And yet, your scowl is gone." The butler scratched the dog's chin. "At least one resident of this house acknowledges my affection."

"Your affection is not unnoticed." Cyril swore under his breath. He'd not meant to sound ungrateful but every sentence turned dark. His eyes flicked to the stack of small journals on the bottom shelf of the bookcase. Brenner had purchased them, stating they weren't ordinary journals but *gratitude journals.* It was a poor attempt to get Cyril to look at the shinier side of life, but even at twelve, Cyril dug in his heels. He'd draw or list things he hated, but Cyril had refused to *count his blessings* as Brenner would say. The memory pulled at Cyril's heart. He was a blasted fool. "I am ... grateful."

Brenner smirked. "Was it truly as wonderful to say as it was to hear?"

"You are insufferable." Cyril groaned.

With his long legs, Brenner stepped directly in front of him. "You cannot ignore the housekeeper or the young widow for long."

"I can ignore any woman for as long as I please." The Darrow pedigree was nothing but lifted chins and low morals. The patriarch lived in the county over. Not far enough for Cyril's liking. He couldn't admit to Brenner that he'd met Lady Darrow on the ridge.

"Do not hold old insults against this lady." Brenner pointed to the card. "She's a widow. And you are a gentleman."

Cyril sniffed again. "I'm no gentleman."

"She's American."

His gaze flicked to the butler. Cyril had only just met the woman an hour earlier. How on earth did Brenner know these little details? "Poor, little John had to cross the pond before he could get a wife."

"She more than likely had no idea what she was being shackled to."

"Her in-laws will have her packed and on her way soon." He tilted his head. "When did he die?"

"A few months ago, maybe less. Maybe more."

Cyril twisted in his chair, wincing at the skin pulling. "And she's still here."

A smile tugged on Brenner's lips. "I do believe the Darrows are frustrated by that fact."

"What do you know?" He narrowed his gaze. Slowly, he stood— Brenner sighed—and Cyril waved about the room. "I'm not walking about. I merely stood."

Brenner was at his side, helping Cyril back to the chair. "She's an heiress. Her father has racing stables back in America."

"Then why the kennels?"

"I believe that was Sir John." Brenner pulled a blanket from the bay window. Leaning over Cyril, he paused.

Cyril grabbed it before his butler could tuck the blanket around him like a child. He would be up and about again tomorrow as if nothing happened. "Again, why is she still here?"

Brenner shrugged. "Perhaps that is why the housekeeper wishes to speak to you."

"Come off it. What did she say?"

He bowed dramatically. "Why, sir, I am but a humble butler. I believe you'll need to answer her call before you'll learn more of her."

Cyril scowled as Brenner left. Mumbling a curse, Cyril froze, catching his reflection in the window. Across his cheeks and forehead were patches of different colors.

He didn't take callers, nor would he. One look would have the lady fainting. He'd seen her, once or twice, on the hill dividing their properties. Her horse was tall with long legs and a refined head. Cyril would never venture farther, nor would he ever speak to her again.

CHAPTER 3

$\mathcal{L}$ady Josephine Darrow

Leaving the station, Josi felt the heaviness in her chest. She'd both received word from her father and posted a letter as well. She'd taken for granted the luxuries of her youth. She'd never worried so much over posting an envelope overseas. The letters, oddly, traveled to New York City's office, where the telegraph would be sent to California. Heaven knew she'd paid a small fortune in postage during her exchange with Sir John before they met. California to Wales was an exorbitant fare, but her father never complained. Sir John had come courting, traveling from New York to Kentucky and then finally out west to California. Josi had accompanied plenty of horses between both coasts, but she'd never loved anything more than her father's farm and the attached racetrack. Not until Sir John tempted her with an easy smile.

Josi wouldn't trust a stranger again. The encounter with the broody earl had Josi questioning her reason for staying in Wales instead of running for home. In truth, his words had her debating everything from her horsemanship to her very residence in the small town on the edge of Wales. She'd confessed to her housekeeper that she'd told her father as much—that she no longer felt compelled to brave out her mourning in Wales. Josi would return home to the warmth of California. It'd take at least a fortnight for her words to travel to her father. She'd been foolish, marrying a man she barely knew and leaving for a country she'd never been.

And now, with Josi's encouragement, her housekeeper would be looking for work. Josi had promised a glowing reference. With boots long past their prime, Josi gave way to the brisk walk to her humble home. California was dry and warm for most of the year, with the farmers and residents fretting about the meager rainfall. She'd once thought Wales a wonderland for how easy and often the storms came.

A month or so would pass before she would receive word from her father. Her pulse began racing. Josi would need to fend off the wolves or she'd lose the remaining chickens and pig. She couldn't afford the next four weeks if she didn't find a solution to the wolves. Those animals were capable of so much more than the foxes in California. Breaking into coops and pigsties was terrifying. The wolves had begun to circle closer to her home after a thief had stolen her husband's shepherds. Josi's pack of guard dogs no longer kept her livestock safe. She and her housekeeper clung together to keep the manor running—and fending off her in-laws from trying to steal her mare.

The sun peeked from behind the dark clouds with the hope of a sunny afternoon. In her front garden, Josi let her head fall back and closed her eyes. The warmth of the sun spilled into her chest. Oh, how she'd missed the blessed sun. Instead of entering her home and speaking with her housekeeper about the future, Josi circled the house and opted for the stables. Not riding on a day this pleasant felt like a sin.

She was out on the meadow between her house and the woods soon enough. Josi didn't bother looking for wolf tracks, not today. Not when the sun could embrace Josi, reminding her of youthful summers. Josi gave the earl's property a wide berth, not eager to repeat their exchange from yesterday.

By the country's standards, Josi was gently bred, but her patience was falling short with the local villagers. Her late husband was not well thought of, and every resident—other than her servants—assigned her the same character.

Her husband's shepherds were stolen shortly after he'd passed, but something was changing. She could feel it in the wind and in the late-night howls. Josi gripped the reins in her hand, a chill creeping up her spine. The earl was correct. The wolf tracks that once kept to the woods were now before her, connecting her property to his.

When Josi had arrived from America several months before, the wolves were a rarity, not a nightly ritual. The occasional howl was carried by the wind from miles away. Narrowing her gaze, Josi's eyes flicked back and forth between the two properties while her mare pawed at the ground impatiently. Josi dismounted and took off her gloves, wanting to feel the muddy paw prints with her hands. She'd watched her father do the same when checking the perimeter of his farm back in the States. Granted, her father raised thoroughbreds not Malinois shepherds.

Josi had been newly wed when Sir John had sped off on her horse, eager to prove his supposedly superior horsemanship. A broken leg and back did not humble him. Nor did the terrifying fevers.

Josi stood and wiped the mud from her hands. The familiar pang of homesickness took over. She was raised by gentle parents without regard to social class or strict protocols. More than once, Josi had been tempted to sail home and bask in the warm rays of a summer sun. She lifted her face to the Welsh sky, rain on the periphery. There was little warmth in Wales. She had hardly set foot in the country and had felt the cold slap of another world.

A wolf howled in the distance. The breeze wrapped around her neck, fanning the growing fear. She'd kept to the house on her rides, staying clear of the woods. She no longer had a dog—or dogs—to run alongside her on her daily adventures.

The wind spun around, stealing the last of her warmth.

Eying a nearby stump, Josi guided her mare toward the impromptu mounting block. She might be tall for a woman, but her horse was a lanky, seventeen-hands high. Sir John had special heels made for his boots to ensure he was taller than Josi. She hadn't minded being the same height until he'd badgered her about her long legs. Her childhood had brought many a jockey to her dinner table— her father a rare horse breeder whose dining table included every employee. A man's—or woman's—frame was an asset, not a weakness.

Her late husband thought himself lucky, snagging an heiress to fill his coffers. He'd been utterly humiliated when he'd waltzed into the bank and found that his wife's family was wealthy while he was not. He'd demanded letter after letter be written to her father. The charming Welsh gent who'd swept her off her feet had disappeared.

The lie didn't sit well. Josi was willing to believe the deceit.

Her sudden engagement to Sir John had little to do with his charm —or lack thereof. She'd lost her dearest friend a few weeks before his arrival. A Welsh gentleman had been a welcome distraction, until she found herself married at the end of a whirlwind courtship. Her blessed father was eager to see her smile but not beguiled enough to hand over a hard-earned fortune. Sir John was uncomfortable around her father or anyone who didn't fawn over a Welsh knight. Her father's quiet way had always calmed her. Josi was one of four daughters, and the only one to travel overseas.

Josi held out her hand. Warmth washed over her at the sight of dirt on her palm. Comfort was found in touching the earth. She patted her mare's neck. The warmth grew. Thousands of miles away, horses dimmed the ache, the longing for home.

Thunder clapped above her. The weather and accents weren't the only foreign concept to her. A rigid class system and strange divide between those with titles and those without was something Josi still struggled with. Horses and trainers had surrounded her childhood. The wealthy in California had earned their fortunes, their daughters raised on farms while the British aristocracy seemed to pride themselves on *not* earning their place in society.

Freya pawed at the ground and, like a toddler, tossed its head in a tantrum. Josi had kept her still too long. As kindred spirits, neither horse nor mistress excelled at being stagnant. She urged her horse forward into a wide-circle canter. Slowly, her mare settled into the rocking rhythm and lowered her head. Josi eased the horse to a sitting trot. She'd come to this very crest a dozen times, but today—*today*—she would venture to her neighbor's property.

Descending the hill, Josi leaned back as they navigated the uneven terrain. She kept her eyes sharp for any evidence of a wolf den. The sheer volume of their howls had Josi believing their den was just outside her bedroom window.

Movement to her right caught Josi's attention. The horse trembled as something moved along the edge of the woods.

A black horse appeared near the woods on the earl's property. Even from a distance, the horse was enormous but not the footman leading the magnificent beast. The earl must not be riding today. Long-legged and black as night, Josi stared at the horse. Freya—just as impressed—called, the neigh rippling through her mare.

"Easy," Josi cooed to Freya. The courage she'd felt just a moment ago to cross over to the earl's property vanished.

Her mare called out again—thunder clapped overhead, drowning its call. Freya danced underneath Josi. A howl split through the air, the wolf much closer.

Josi urged her mare forward. She'd put off this moment long enough; she would not let a single wolf deter her. She needed the earl's help. The prints near her home demanded action. Keeping the wolves at bay should be under the reclusive castle's jurisdiction. The man was an earl after all.

Despite living in Wales the past few years, neither Josi nor her horse was used to the wet weather. Winter or summer, rain fell and the world darkened. Lightning flashed across the sky. The mare hopped in place, nervous energy curling up and around her. Another clap of thunder. Her mare spun around, nearly unseating Josi. Rain would arrive in mere minutes. Blast it all. She could do one more circle, but a visit with the earl would have to wait.

CHAPTER 4

*C*yril Heathclove, Lord Fennyson

From his perch in his study, Cyril caught the profile of a female servant marching toward the front garden. This must have been the housekeeper Brenner had spoken of. Cyril slipped from the room, escaping to the stables, a slight limp to his walk. He'd sent his footman to walk his geldings, but perhaps Cyril should be riding instead of nursing his wounds. The blasted cut was healing well enough, but he would not be caught at home. Brenner would not let Cyril avoid Lady Darrow forever; the butler was far too well-mannered for Cyril's liking. There was a reason Cyril never attended to his duties in Parliament or frequented London. He much preferred the reclusive Welsh woods. The quiet demeanor of his horses grounded Cyril, inviting his trust like his country never had.

Cyril saddled his stallion, refusing the help of a groomsman who'd just brought the horse in from a walk. The fewer servants he had, the less people stared at him. He waited a few moments on the path leading toward the woods. On his way home from the post station, Cyril had watched Lady Darrow enter her front garden. Perhaps she'd heeded his words on not taking such a green horse out near the woods. The mare couldn't be more than four or five years. The conformation and gait were impressive, but what use was a pretty thing when all it did was shiver with fear? Cyril preferred the rugged mind of his Percherons, steady and loyal. They could work the fields, pull his carriage, or carry him toward the wolves without question. Lady Darrow's mare could inspire a whistle or win a race, but it would surely break Lady Darrow's neck before the year was through.

Urging Atlas forward, Cyril kept his eye on the ridge. He'd felt reluctant to leave her yesterday. He could blame his noble upbringing, but there was something more—or perhaps unnerving her with his gruff words gave him a bit of joy. Brenner was immune to Cyril's antics and did not blush delightfully when frustrated.

Would the widow be daft enough to return to the woods? Her housekeeper had come knocking twice each day, but Cyril stayed in his study. He didn't need another rumor in the village. Every man—or woman—did the same initial gasp, followed by fumbling apologies after one look at his face. Each time felt like the first, another wound to his pride.

When he was a child, his mother would fuss, telling Cyril just how handsome of a lad he was. Her slight Scottish lilt couldn't soften the stares. A misshapen face *was* a shock. Only those who'd known him since boyhood stopped noticing the scars; the number of trusted people was frighteningly small.

Atlas began climbing the ridge instead of heading toward the woods. The horse must have sensed Cyril's curiosity. This feeling, the unsettling of Cyril's nerves couldn't be worry. Cyril didn't concern himself with the feelings of the villagers or neighbors and certainly not the wife of Sir John. But the wolves were becoming braver, coming closer and closer to both his property and Lady Darrow's. Their appetites were growing fierce and they were doubling their numbers. He'd seen them go into a frenzy over a pigeon. If Lady Darrow fell near their den, death would be certain. Cyril had filed a petition to the villagers, but no one paid him heed. He was not only the town monster, but the village curmudgeon as well. They had no idea the personal cost of his speaking to strangers and their reaction to his butchered face. He'd thought saving the animals, the livelihood of many townsfolk, was worth the risk. But yet again, his word meant nothing.

Cyril had tried to trap the wolves, but they smelled his scent. He felt a deep well of guilt for the terror—after all, it was his father who'd tried to breed the blasted wolves. Sir John had tried to do the same, mixing the Shepherds in. But wolves weren't dogs. There was a savage nature about them, a yearning to return to the wild of their ancestors.

His father had believed in the necessity of wolves, a balance of prey and predators. Cyril had seen the balance tip when Sir John foolishly began his half-hearted kennel. He'd discovered both men's endeavors by accident. He was ten when Cyril followed his father out to the woods.

Cyril hadn't planned on going far, but a few paces into the woods, he caught a glimpse of his father's shirt and the tail of the shepherd. Both man and beast were digging under a tree next to the stream. Cyril didn't call out to him but kept to the shadows like Brenner had taught him.

His father stood and went deeper into the thick foliage, stopping every few feet to look at the holes. The wind was sharp and the air cold as they plunged deeper into the forest, but Cyril refused to turn back, curiosity nipping at his heels.

But then his father disappeared. A rush of growls and yips, like his shepherd but deeper.

Cyril silently walked between the thick foliage and trees until he saw the crevice between a fallen tree trunk and enormous stone. He crept closer to the narrow opening when his father burst through, a puppy squirming in his arms.

Terrified at his father's temper, Cyril tucked his head and ran straight home, ignoring the calls of his mother from her reading room. It was hours before his father came to his bed, Cyril still trembling, waiting for the worst.

"You followed me," his father had said in a low voice, shutting the door. He'd done this before, after Cyril had disappointed him. "Why?"

Cyril had stared up at the broad shoulders of his father. Both father and son were spitting images of each other, or so Cyril was often told. "I ... only ... I ..."

His father released a sigh and sat on the edge of the bed, the wood groaning under the weight. "Does your mother know?"

Cyril shook his head.

"There's a balance, Cyril." His father folded his muscled arms. "Wolves are needed, but if we can domesticate a few, I think our village would be better for it. We cannot control what we don't understand."

The severity in his words and the question about his mother had given a silent warning; no one must know of his father's adventures. It'd taken another decade before Cyril realized his father had slowly bred shepherds in with the wolves. The new wolf breed hadn't changed their nature. They still developed a healthy fear of the village and kept to the woods. But something had shifted in recent months, and the wolves were no longer afraid.

Atlas' ears flicked to the widow's home. Lady Darrow was cantering her long-legged mare into a large circle. She was mad. No one with a firm grip on reality would be so foolish, especially on such a flighty horse.

Cyril pushed back the thoughts of Lady Darrow that seemed to intrude more and more—thoughts of how her delightful blush could make a man's heart beat fast. Thoughts of how, in just a few moments of meeting her, he was aware of her presence, and he felt the urge to warn her, to protect her but not enough to speak to her as a gentleman. Or remove his hat.

Lady Darrow was just another woman, another lady to turn her nose at him. Her dark hair and clear blue eyes ensured she'd marry again. Her children would cling to her as Cyril had to his own mother. Her skin had turned crimson with embarrassment, but her eyes held a fire, a reckless flame—Cyril would burn if he got too close. She already resented him helping her home yesterday. Truthfully, he'd loved every minute of riling her.

Cyril pulled Atlas back. He would stick to his property, watching Lady Darrow from afar.

A distant howl pierced the air. The wolves were awake. The afternoon was just beginning, but with the sun hiding behind the clouds, the animals would be emboldened.

Lady Darrow kept her canter, appearing completely unaware of the danger. Cyril watched her, concern giving way to frustration. No one took him seriously. He didn't speak for the pleasure of hearing his own voice. There was a reason he'd helped the widow. The gesture was not with affection. He'd hated her coward of a husband.

There was a kilometer or two between them with wolf tracks littering the ground. Despite his and Atlas' frame, they wouldn't be in her line of vision unless she came toward the ridge. Once Lady Darrow rounded the west end of her circle, she'd see Cyril. Perhaps there was a way to teach the foolish woman a lesson.

A wolf howled, another answered. In long strides, Atlas covered the ground and perched on the ridge. The mare hopped, then reared, tossing Lady Darrow. She fell to the rocky meadow. A frightening crack pierced the air.

CHAPTER 5

*L*ady Josephine Darrow

Blue. The sky was blue. A man's face appeared, covering the sky. His eyes were dark, nearly black. Patches of different skin tones appeared to be sewn together on his face and neck, the scars old. She stared, unable to look away. He was speaking to her—she must know him. His voice was garbled. Josi tried to sit up but winced, her head and back throbbing.

The man's brow furrowed, and he kneeled next to her. "Lady Darrow—"

"Lady Darrow ..." She'd heard that name before.

Sighing, the man leaned over, searching her face and torso. His shoulders were broad. Her pulse quickened. He sank back and ran his massive hands down his face, his eyes flicking to something next to Josi. "Your horse has run off."

"Does my father know?" A feeling of longing—a yearning for home —came over her. The thought surprised her. She'd just seen her father a moment before. He would be chasing her filly.

"What is the last thing you remember?" the man asked, his voice low and firm. An accent. His hands gently touched her forehead and neck, reminding Josi of her father nursing her after a fall.

"I fell, didn't I?" There was a familiarity in the man's eyes, but Josi couldn't remember his name. Nor could she remember the question he just asked. Her stomach twisted. Her vision blurred. She rolled over, dry heaving on the wet grass. The moment passed; her stomach quieted.

Josi stared at the long-stemmed weeds and grass. Her fingers wrapped around a stem. She was used to the soft, low grass of California. She had to be in Virginia—no. That wasn't right.

The sound of fabric ripping pulled her attention back to the man. He wiped her mouth with a ripped cloth. "Do y'know where you are?" There was a sing-song melody in his words.

"No." Josi tried sitting up, but he shook his head.

"Not yet."

"You're British." That felt right. Josi had been writing to a foreign gentleman—or maybe he'd already arrived. She couldn't remember. A flutter of panic. She'd forgotten his name. "I know you."

He nodded, his eyes softening. "We've met."

"I can't remember." Her cheeks flushed with heat. He was kind like her father. "Apologies."

His lips stretched to a crooked grin, a glint of mischief in his eyes. "Cyril."

"Cyril." Pursing her lips, Josi thought long and hard, but no, she couldn't remember the name. The panic returned. "Do you know me as Josi or Josephine?"

"Josi, of course." He winked but looked off to the left as someone approached. "Her horse ran off toward its stable. Send a footman to find the mare. I'll need help getting her up on Atlas. She's dizzy, and I don't dare let her mount on her own."

Cyril's tone was familiar. She *did* know this man, but she thoroughly disliked being talked about. She was quite literally in front of him. She could mount a horse on her own, thank you very much.

"I'm fine." She sat up and gasped—the earth seemed to spin. She squeezed her eyes shut, refusing to sink back down. "I ... can ride."

Even to her own ears, Josi sounded doubtful. Opening her eyes, she gazed up the darkening sky and inhaled. She smelled of horses and felt the warmth of the sun. Everything felt right—and wrong.

"Blast it, woman, you're not meant to sit up so fast." Cyril's arm went behind her back. He was a strange and moody man. He must have just come from Britain, his accent thick. "I told you not to ride that mare."

"You told me ..." A flicker of familiarity. She'd been writing to a man from Wales. The memory was fuzzy. Josi nodded—slowly as to not reignite the nausea.

"Yes," he growled, his voice almost animal-like. "You've no business riding a horse like that."

"A horse like that?" Josi snapped, her head clearing. Her father had taught her to ride as soon as Josi'd learned to walk. "I'm an accomplished—"

"Liar." His eyes narrowed.

"How dare you—"

He palmed his forehead. "You've fallen and hit your head."

The words were a hiss, cutting through Josi. She could see the depths of his gaze, his eyes dark and stormy. She scowled.

"How accomplished can you—"

"Stop." Josi winced, her head in her hands.

"Oh, *argylwyddes.*" He pulled her hands from her head.

"My name is Josi." Her head ached. A tear fell down her cheek. She jerked her hand from his.

Cyril's eyes widened, surprised at her vehemence.

She struggled to a stand. His arm went around her back. Pushing away from him, Josi saw the ridge—the divide between her land and his. Memories pieced together, and her heart sank. She was Lady Darrow, the widow. "You're the earl."

The concern in his eye vanished, a stoic expression washing over. "You're hurt."

"You're a liar." They were not friends. He wouldn't call her Josi. Panic settled on her shoulders. *Leave*—safety was not with a stranger. With wobbling steps, Josi shuffled down the path. She couldn't remember falling or riding her mare, but she would not stay here. *Freya.* Her horse was nowhere to be found. The earl had admitted as much.

His footsteps thundered after her, fanning her fear. Lord Fennyson's stride was much longer than hers. Her pulse raced. It might be midday but Josi was alone. With a man. Other than the threat of wolves, she'd never been more afraid.

Lord Fennyson cut in front her, forcing a sudden halt. Her boot caught on a rock. His arm shot out, steadying her. The earl's height loomed over her. "You need rest," he said with a low rumble.

"No." A lump formed in her throat. *I need my father.* Her face flushed with embarrassment. The fall had pushed her emotions to the surface. The brute in front of her was everything that Josi hated about Wales. He was dark, cold, and unforgiving.

"I'm taking you home. A physician will tend to you." His words were like ice and fire on her skin, both competing for dominance.

Looking into his hard gaze, Josi whispered, "Is that a threat?"

"Mr. Thatcher is a physician, *argylwyddes.*" A vein throbbed on his neck. The absurdity was oddly comforting to Josi. "D'you think I'd send for a butcher?"

Josi lifted her chin. The earl could drag her wherever he liked, but she wasn't leaving anywhere without her horse.

"You are not my husband, nor are you my father," she said in a thin voice. Her legs began shaking. Standing wouldn't be an option for very long. A dark storm brewed in his eyes, his brow furrowing. She couldn't act the coward now. "My duty is to find my horse."

The harshness in Lord Fennyson's features dissolved, leaving only soft concern. He exhaled and searched her face, his warm breath on her skin. Under his scrutiny, Josi felt an urge to lean forward, to breathe in the scent of him. Her stomach churned. She swallowed hard.

"I've several men looking for her." Lord Fennyson's gaze was still supple, tender. "We might be strangers but know that I would not leave a horse to the wolves. Nor an *argylwyddes.*"

"An *argylwyddes?*"

Gently, he whispered, "A lady."

Josi blinked to clear her dizzying mind. The softness in his voice tempted her. Her pulse slowed, her skin prickled. Lord Fennyson grasped the stallion's reins with one hand, then held out his other to her.

"Trust me, Josi." The way he said her name sent a warm shiver along her skin.

She should correct him, demand the earl address her as Lady Darrow, but said nothing, placing her hand in his. He boosted her up on the horse. Her hands immediately grasped the thick, black mane. The height dizzied her once more. In one graceful movement, Lord Fennyson swung up behind her. He reached around her to take up the reins, trapping Josi against his body. She should move away but found herself leaning back to stave off the nausea. A strange feeling of safety, an emotion she'd not felt since she arrived in Wales, enveloped her.

His stallion carefully picked its way down the ridge toward the earl's stables. Away from hers. The flicker of panic returned. She was leaving her horse and entering the den of the earl. She'd heard the rumors. She stiffened and tried to sit up. The less contact she had, the better. Her pulse began racing, her breath shortened. The ride was intimate in a way she never was with Sir John. Her late husband would not have touched her forehead or insisted on her seeing a physician. Nothing in her short, married life was like this gentle ride with Lord Fennyson.

Her cheeks rushed with heat—she was blushing, again. Not until this moment had Josi realized just how precarious her predicament was; she was a widow. The nearest male relative was miles away, and yet ... the way the earl's breath stirred her hair, the way his chest radiated heat against her back, and the way his muscled arms jostled against Josi as the horse wound its way through rocks ...

A wolf's howl split the air, sending a shudder down her spine. Lord Fennyson tensed. Another wolf answered. Josi's head throbbed, her chest tightened.

"Hold on, Josi," Lord Fennyson whispered in her ear.

CHAPTER 6

yril Heathclove, Lord Fennyson

With both his arms holding Lady Darrow upright, Cyril urged Atlas forward. She groaned and lay back against him. In great strides, Atlas covered the ground, wolves howling behind them.

Just as his back gate came into view, Cyril slowed. He'd planned a day of hunting the wolf pack, but his schedule had been promptly— and properly—sidetracked. Cyril couldn't remember the last time he'd been thoroughly distracted by such an intriguing creature. The stubborn pride Lady Darrow had displayed just a day before was gone, but the need to tease, to elicit a reaction—*any* reaction—from Lady Darrow held Cyril's whole focus.

His horse had carried Cyril and Lady Darrow with deceptive ease, its ears flicking at each wolf howl. The stallion was waiting for the cue to gallop the last bit, but the woman in Cyril's arms was far too dizzy for anything more than a stroll. From the bump on the back of her head, she'd taken quite the fall, and Mr. Thatcher should be at the manor by the time they arrived. The memory of her face, confused and dizzy, was a moment Cyril would remember. She didn't shrink or gasp at his patched skin. Her mind finally cleared, and he'd waited for the shock. Nothing.

He was positively entranced by her. Not in decades had someone been so unaffected by his misshapen face.

Cyril glanced down. Her black hair tumbled down around her shoulders. Like his mother, Lady Darrow had undoubtedly spent hours with her maid that morning. Lady Darrow stared straight ahead, her back slowly leaning toward him. Her body relaxed. Her hand slipped, landing on his leg. He held his breath. He'd not been physically close with a woman. Between his face and temper, Cyril had a skill for repelling friends and intimidating enemies.

At the tender age of twelve—the morning he saw the first of his skin to fade—he'd accompanied his parents to the village festival and danced with several young girls around his age. He'd felt awkward and unsure. Not like this.

The simple touch of her back against his chest warmed him. An ache he didn't know existed cracked open deep within. Her hand on his thigh was tiny, helpless. *Helpless.* The Lady Darrow from yesterday would rather throttle Cyril than ask for help.

Just outside the back garden fence, Atlas sidestepped the uneven ground, managing to avoid the gorse and the low oak branches. A hoof caught on a rock, jostling them both. Lady Darrow's nails dug into his leg.

Brenner rushed from the house in long strides, housekeeper and footman in tow. He came to Atlas's side with the strength of a young man, not a butler twice Cyril's age. "Mr. Thatcher's inside."

"And my horse?" Lady Darrow asked.

Pride swelled in Cyril's chest. Few men and even fewer women cared about their horses enough to fret this much. There was a strength in Lady Darrow—*Josi.* He'd thought to tease her a bit before her head cleared. Cyril had done his fair share of falling, letting his attic for rent for a while afterward, until his head cleared and he became master of his own mind again. His mood had lifted when her brow furrowed adorably as she looked up at him in confusion. For the first time, a woman stared up at him, not in horror but in wonder. He'd hold the memory of her ice blue eyes for a while yet.

"Don't move," Cyril whispered, unable to conceal his concern. His worry came as a shock. He didn't know this woman nor did he hold any regard for her. She had been married to the foozler Sir John. And yet, his hand covered hers and gave a reassuring squeeze.

With a slow nod, Lady Darrow answered, "I'll not move."

Careful to move the saddle as little as possible, Cyril dismounted.

"By jove, you're enormous," she murmured, her eyes flicking from his shoulders to the horse.

In an instant, Cyril was an awkward young lad with arms and legs too long for graceful movements. "Afraid there's nothing I can do about that part."

Her lips quirked into a smile. A light sparkled in her eyes. "You're the first man I've met that hasn't made a comment about my own height."

"You're the first woman I've met who didn't gasp at my face." The words hung between them. He'd not meant to speak them out loud. Brenner froze beside him. Cyril had breached a silent vow to never discuss the patched skin.

She narrowed her eyes and stared intently at his face. Embarrassment gave way to frustration, then anger began welling inside of Cyril. He'd been nothing but kind to the hare-brained woman. How dare she insult him so blatantly. He leaned in and opened his mouth when she tilted her head and asked, "What kind of stitching did they use?"

"What kind of—"

Pointing to her elbow, she drew a line down her sleeve. She reached for him with one hand. "The stitches near your chin are like mine in my arm, but the stitches around your cheek are like—" Her cheeks flushed as her other hand touched her hip.

The anger melted away as her blush deepened. What an intriguing creature indeed. Cyril leaned in. "Like what?"

"Nothing." She shook her head, then paled.

Cyril winced, remembering the nauseas of a head injury. Stepping closer, he wrapped his right arm around her waist, and she braced herself against his left arm. She leaned into him, her hair spilling against his neck and chest. Just as her boots touched the ground, she glanced up. Her eyes held his gaze, and he paused, unable to think, unable to move. Curiosity and stubbornness swirled within the icy blue eyes of Lady Darrow—and something more. Grief. Cyril knew sorrow and was quite acquainted with loss. Shame washed over him. He'd bullied this poor woman who'd left her native country and lost her husband. She was a widow grieving the loss of a beloved spouse.

"Lady Darrow!" A familiar woman in a smart, navy dress came rushing toward them. Cyril couldn't place how he knew her. The woman's hair was gently turning to gray at her temples, and the beginning of wrinkles outlined her eyes and lips. Gems were sewn along the neckline and rings glittered on her fingers. Dark circles underlined her heavy eyes.

Lady Darrow stiffened, her nails biting his hand.

"She needs to lie down." Cyril nodded to Brenner. His butler would need to distract whoever this visitor was while Cyril assisted Lady Darrow inside. With his lips against her ear, he whispered, "I'm going to pick you up. It might help to close your eyes."

Obediently, she squeezed her eyes shut as he gathered her against him. She groaned, her pallor becoming more sickly. Not until she was in his arms, legs folded and arms tucked, did Cyril realize just how tall she was. Like his father, Cyril was built like a Percheron, several inches taller than the average man, while Lady Darrow was similar to her mare, lean and lithe.

"Lord Fennyson." With a hand on her hip, the woman in navy stepped in front of Cyril. The jewels sewn into the neckline were not sapphires but paste, and the rings adorning her fingers were colored glass. This woman was a pretender. "A carriage is waiting out front—"

"Move aside," Cyril ordered. He didn't know this imposter nor would he entertain her a moment longer.

Narrowing her shrewd gaze, the woman tightened her grip on his sleeve. "As her nearest relative, I am worried about her wellbeing."

Lady Darrow grimaced in his arms. Cyril shifted her weight,

careful to keep her head higher than her body. "I don't care who you're related to. This woman was hurt on my property and needs to be seen by a physician. You can move aside or be moved. The choice is yours."

The woman's face darkened, and her lips trembled. "When my son fell, did you bother to look after him?"

Pieces of his memory fell into place. "Sir John." Blast it all, Lady Greyen had descended to the lowly sphere of Cyril's company.

Groaning, Lady Darrow twisted, coughing and heaving—she was about to retch once more. Cyril brushed passed Lady Greyen and burst into the house, Lady Darrow writhing in his arms.

CHAPTER 7

*L*ady Josephine Darrow

Gripping Lord Fennyson's collar, Josi fought the urge to vomit. She could not—would *not*—lose control of her faculties in front of Lady Greyen. Josi felt every inch of the familiar condemnation. According to Sir John's family, she was an American, a savage from a lawless land. Even Lord Fennyson thought Josi's mind was addled—riding her spirited mare alone. *Cyril.* The temptation to use his given name grew. The shock of her mother-in-law following the earl would be well worth the effort.

Lord Fennyson was a curious man, a walking irony of gentle and gruff. He laid Josi on a chaise sofa and propped her torso and head with pillows. One moment, he was tender, endearing—so much like her father—and the next minute, he scowled and pouted like a toddler. Leaning over her, Lord Fennyson cradled one arm under her, the other adjusting the pillows. His face inches from hers, he whispered, "Is that comfortable, or should I add more?"

She opened her mouth to speak. A wave of emotion fell over her. She couldn't tell if it was a pang of homesickness or if she was just a pathetic woman so starved for affection that the slightest kindness threatened to undo her. She was not a silly schoolgirl.

Worry lined his features as he searched her face. Flecks of gold were in his eyes, so dark they appeared black. A smattering of freckles dotted the dark patches of skin on his cheeks. The scars from the stitches reminded her of home. Like most of her fellow daughters of racing stables, she'd learned to stitch skin instead of the pretty needle-point art of the *ton*. A warmth filled her, the nausea subsiding. The structure of his jaw, cheeks and nose pricked her heart. Like her father, he was undoubtedly a handsome man before the injury. A lump formed in her throat. By jove, Josi missed her family.

But her father would never interfere, leaving the decision to her. He'd not liked her marrying a Welshman but held his tongue. He stiffened every time Sir John entered the room but was polite and kind. He'd thought the long-distance writing would eventually fizzle, a passing fancy. The closest thing to dissent was his final words to her before boarding the train toward New York. *You don't need a title to know your worth. You're a lady in your own right. I'll not transfer your share of winnings until you're certain Wales is worthy of you.*

For years, her father had quietly tucked a percentage of the horse winnings in her name. Josi didn't truly deserve them. She didn't train the young ones, but she had a knack for quieting the nervous horses, especially in transit. Pride had kept her from asking for funds. Her father had done the same, refusing money from his father to start his stock.

She reached out, her fingers tracing the stitches on the earl's cheek. His eyes widened.

"What manner of sin is this?" The shrill voice of Lady Greyen pierced the room.

Josi froze—her hand on Lord Fennyson's cheek. Her face and neck went hot. She dropped her hand and tucked her chin in embarrassment. She didn't know what had happened. Lord Fennyson was a stranger—worse, he was a Welshman, and his lot was not to be trusted. He would toss Josi out at any moment. She hugged herself, the nausea returning. If she didn't have her mare, Josi would have boarded the next train for home. Towing a horse halfway across the world was an exorbitant expense. *We could have built a house for that amount,* Sir John would frequently moan at the end of each month. But her father wanted her to have at least one friend, one familiarity in a foreign country. He'd not complained about the expense for his daughter.

"What has possessed you to lose your moral compass?" Lady Greyen's rapid footsteps echoed in the dark study.

"She fell and hit her head." Lord Fennyson's voice boomed. He'd not retreated from Josi nor had he exactly defended her.

Shame washed over her. For once, Lady Greyen was correct to criticize. The earl was a stranger. Why couldn't Josi remember that fact? His accent and broody nature were nothing like her father. There was no reason for Josi's compulsion to touch him. Perhaps her fall had knocked all sense from her. Her touch had felt right. Natural even. Only a woman who'd lost her senses would think that.

The earl stood to his full height. A draft came over Josi, the chill reminding her that she was very much alone. A fortnight. She need only last a little longer before her father would receive her telegraph. Hope brought warmth.

Lady Greyen came to the chaise. "And what were the two of you doing that she would hit her head?"

"Are you accusing me of being untoward?" Towering over the woman, Lord Fennyson's expression was unreadable. Tension filled the room in a heavy rush.

Holding up two fingers, Lady Greyen hissed. "Two months. My son has been buried only two months." She flicked her wrist at Josi's dark green riding habit. "You've not even bothered to mourn him."

Josi winced. She hadn't meant to disrespect the dead. She'd known she was to wear mourning clothes, but there wasn't money to provide the necessary black clothing. Secretly—selfishly—Sir John's death was a relief. She'd grieved the marriage long before he passed away. She'd innocently thought every man would be like her father, that love was a given not a rarity.

Her hands clenching into tight fists, Lady Greyen looked more like a frustrated child than a grieving mother. "You seem all too happy to be rid of him, throwing yourself into the arms of someone like—"

"Someone like what?" His voice was deceptively calm, but his arms were taut. Lord Fennyson looked ready to pounce.

"Do not twist my words." The baroness lifted her chin. "There's not been peace between our homes in years."

The sound of padded paws was followed by a dog's low growl. An enormous gray shepherd paused between Lord Fennyson and Lady Greyen, its head pivoting between the two. The face was shaped like the Malinois Shepherds Sir John had tried to breed—the same shepherds that were stolen after he died. Suspicion swept across Josi's neck.

"Lord Fennyson!" A hunched man with a few wisps of white hair entered the room, a black medicine bag tucked under his arm.

Lady Greyen's gaze flicked from the shepherd to the older man. "Who is—?"

Clasping hands with Lord Fennyson, the old man's eyes lit with joy. His neck craned to see the earl. "Have you injured yourself so quickly?"

The affection from the physician changed Lord Fennyson, and his lips stretched into a smile. A light sparked in his eyes. "Not this time. Lady Darrow has fallen from her horse." He palmed the back of his head. Lord Fennyson's aura had shifted completely, light touching each word. "She earns good marks for the size of the bump."

"Ah, so you've spread your knack of falling to your friends, have you?" Before the earl could answer, the good doctor turned to Lady Greyen. "And you must be the mother? Don't you worry. She'll be good as new."

"I am not her mother." Lady Greyen sniffed and sidestepped the doctor. "That horse should have been put down. It's as dangerous as its owner."

Lord Fennyson wedged his enormous frame between the doctor and Lady Greyen. "She lost her whereabouts for a few minutes and retched twice."

"Ah." The doctor nodded and gave a once over, gently touching Josi's head and neck. "And does the damsel in distress have a name?"

"Oh, careful, Thatcher." Lord Fennyson playfully *tsk*ed. "Lady

Darrow doesn't take kindly to pandering. I tried helping her yesterday, and she'd rather strangle me than listen."

Cupping her mouth, Josi whispered loudly to the doctor, "He wasn't helping; he was ordering."

The doctor winked at her. "He doesn't know the way of things." He pointed to the simple wedding band on his finger and, with a voice warm with age, added, "I take my orders from the missus. She tells me just how to help."

Lady Greyen paced behind the earl, shaking her head. She was only one of many opinions in her household. Her overbearing nature was similar to her son—and husband. Sir John commanded; his word was law. Falling from her mare didn't stop his tongue from firing barbs. When Lady Greyen came rushing to his side, they laid fault at Josi's feet. Even Josi's housekeeper—as kind as she was—still bowed to Lady Greyen's every whim.

"We'll need to keep your head and neck elevated." With a warm smile and crinkled eyes, Mr. Thatcher checked Josi's eyes, pulse, and the bump on her head. "Lord Fennyson, she'll need blankets for her extremities." Turning back to Josi, he added, "You might go into a bit of shock, and your legs and arms will need to be kept warm. It could be a day, or maybe a week, before the world stops turning on you."

Every word felt like a tonic to Josi. Tucking her chin, she broke her gaze. It'd been too long since she'd been taken care of. She'd not realized how privileged her life was before Wales. Naïve, Josi had thought all men would stop to hear her opinion or tease a smile from her. The gentle back and forth of a conversation—no barbs or defensiveness, just a person with words—was how her parents had raised her. But Sir John and his mother thought her a savage, missing vital rules and decorum.

"She'll be well rested in my care." Lady Greyen's shrill words had Josi wincing. "I'll send a footman to take care of that horse."

"*That horse* is on my property, Lady Greyen." The light in Lord Fennyson's eyes dimmed. He had a way of unfurling himself to fill the room, his voice booming. "I do believe poaching is still a crime."

"Poaching?" Lady Greyen's mouth fell open. "It's a horse. A wicked, ill-tempered beast that killed my son. And injured his wife, not that she fulfilled her duties—"

"Good day, Lady Greyen." Lord Fennyson turned from her, seemingly oblivious to the deafening silence falling on the room. His cut was sharp, dismissing the baroness from his presence.

Not that she fulfilled her duties. Josi winced at the words. There was little love lost between Josi and her mother-in-law, but not even Sir John had spoken so sharply to Lady Greyen. The woman was ushered from the room, her shrill voice screaming at the injustice.

The shepherd came to the earl's side, pushing its head against his hand. The simple gesture softened Lord Fennyson in an instant.

Mr. Thatcher leaned over and whispered softly, "Lord Fennyson will always protect his friends."

Peering up at the kind man, Josi whispered, "We're not friends."

"Yet." The doctor grinned widely and winked. "You're not friends, yet."

CHAPTER 8

 yril Heathclove, Lord Fennyson

Cyril paused in front of his study, not yet ready to speak with Lady Darrow. He'd escorted the gentle Mr. Thatcher to his carriage and, earlier, the blasted Lady Greyen.

The taunts from his childhood came back in a flood of painful memories. The baroness and her fool of a son had been the worst of the lot. Their chins lifted, they believed in their own superiority, ignoring Cyril's higher rank. When he could no longer hide the pale patches of his skin, the whispers began. Lady Greyen was giddy at the prospect of Cyril being valued less than her spoiled son. As a boy, Cyril was a future earl and grandson of a duke, but all Cyril wanted was a friend.

Brenner cleared his throat, announcing his presence in the corridor. "Shall I get the door for you, my lord?"

"I hope you've recovered from Lady Greyen's abuse." Cyril hated that woman's wicked tongue. She treated everyone, servant and friend, with the same venom.

"She is determined to find Lady Darrow's horse." Brenner stepped forward, his hand on the doorknob. A sly grin crept along his face, mischief in his eyes. "And, of course, to remove Lady Darrow from your clutches."

Shaking his head, Cyril sighed. "Lady Darrow will be struggling to keep anything down. She's no business traveling anywhere."

Brenner arched an eyebrow. A plan was hatching in his mind. "Lady Greyen lives not far from here."

Cyril rubbed the back of his neck. His world consisted of his horses and servants, leaving little room for other people. He'd not entertained this many visitors in decades. "Speak plainly."

"Her mare is in your stables."

"And?" Cyril had made that happen.

"The horse is safe."

Groaning, Cyril sighed, patience not his virtue. "Blast it, Brenner, say what's on your mind."

"There's no reason for Lady Darrow to remain in your study." Brenner shrugged and motioned to the door. "You could wash your hands of her."

"And give her to the dragon?" Cyril's butler had lost his mind. Lady Darrow would never recover in Lady Greyen's clutches. "The baroness doesn't want her to rest, she wants her to suffer."

Brenner sobered and quietly asked, "Then it begs the question, Lord Fennyson, why do you care?"

"I don't." And he meant it. Cyril was doing his duty as a gentleman, nothing more. Nothing less. "I don't," he added, louder.

Brenner searched Cyril before giving a nod. "I am merely the humble servant."

"She's the wife of that damnable man. I wouldn't give a fig if she rotted or not."

Holding up both hands, Brenner backed away. "I stand corrected, Lord Fennyson."

Cyril's heart pounded in his chest. He didn't care. She was just a woman. She was a pretty thing—he'd give her that—but that was all. There was nothing more to this than an inconvenient accident. Lady Darrow would be back in her home soon enough, battling Lady Greyen while Cyril searched for wolves.

"I'll see that she is comfortable if you need to retire." Tucking one hand behind his back, Brenner leaned over and placed his other hand on the doorknob. "You need not distress yourself over her."

"Move aside," Cyril murmured.

His butler was acting out of sorts, and Cyril would have none of it. He entered the study and took in the room as if for the first time. He'd not had a stranger in his home, let alone in his study, in years. The curtains were outdated, remnants of when his grandfather was his age. His own father refused to update the place, eager to inherit the castle in the north. Except for the novels. Books were lined on the shelves—all of them read or purchased in decades. Cyril had learned the safest way to experience people was through the written word. He was safer tangling with horses and wolves than with criticism from his countrymen—and women.

Her back to Cyril, Lady Darrow was propped up on the chaise, his dog's head in her lap. She stroked behind its ears and traced the dog's eyes and snout. An absent smile was on her lips. When she stopped moving, the dog scooted its head forward, begging for more affection. Her index finger traced the star on Beowulf's forehead.

"Traitor." Cyril moved a chair close to the chaise. He was supposed to just check on the woman, not pull up a chair. There was a draw toward this widow. She possessed an air of innocence with sadness sprinkled in. The history between the Darrow's manor and his own was tentative at best. He'd never cared to cross the ridge and speak to her before now. Her hair spilled forward, and he felt the oddest sensation to lean over and tuck the strand behind her ear. He didn't understand it, and yet, he pulled his chair closer.

Lady Darrow stopped petting the dog, her brow furrowing. His heart sank. While her presence pricked his curiosity, his nearness seemed to unsettle her. Beowulf whimpered and scooted closer, determined to steal Lady Darrow's affection once more.

"I was calling Beowulf the traitor, not you." The words came awkward. He'd much prefer to listen to her brassy American accent than his own Welsh words. "She normally doesn't like anyone. Other than me and Brenner."

Lady Darrow didn't relax. She glanced from him to the door. "I didn't mean to impose."

Blast. She'd heard Cyril's conversation with Brenner. "You're not."

She arched an eyebrow and gave a doubtful look. "You and … Sir John. You two had a history."

"We did."

Lady Darrow swallowed hard. Her gaze flicked to his, a question in her eyes. "You were not friends."

"We were not." Cyril felt compelled to ease her hesitation, unsure of her sudden shyness. She'd nearly touched his face earlier, but now her fingers twisted nervously in her lap.

"Is that why you stole his dogs?"

"His dogs?" Cyril recoiled. "Why would I steal his dogs?"

She began petting Beowulf once more. "This is a Malinois shepherd."

"She's a mix. Half wolf, half shepherd." Cyril didn't need to steal from Sir John. That man gambled or drank away anything of worth. "She's from my father's line."

"Your father?" Her eyes narrowed. "Several weeks ago, every shepherd was stolen from the kennel."

Cyril waved a hand in the air. The *argylwyddes* hadn't a clue the history of the sleepy village. "Beowulf is four years old. Your idiotic husband wasn't breeding until this year."

"Why would Sir John breed shepherds if your—"

"I've no idea why Sir John would do anything. He's never been accused of being clever." His voice rose, turning to a shout. He'd hated the blasted man when he was alive and, for some reason, the idea that he married the creature on the chaise ignited a fire in him. "That man wouldn't know a good decision if it invited him over for tea."

"He's never made a good decision …" She swallowed hard, her eyes drifting to the ring on her hand.

"Blast." A fool, Cyril was nothing but a fool. "Lady Darrow." He leaned over and placed a hand on hers. The sorrow etched in her features pricked his heart. He was the dragon, his tongue wicked and full of fire. "I meant to slight Sir John, not you. Marrying—"

"Was not a good decision." She kept her gaze on her lap, unable to look him in the eye. The silence squeezed his heart. He'd misread and mistreated the woman, blaming her instead of Sir John. "My father was too gentle to forbid me. I didn't know there could be such sadness." She pursed her lips, waiting a beat before continuing. "I thought marriage was just that, a love between two people. Kindness. Warmth. I didn't know there was any other way."

CHAPTER 9

*L*ady Josephine Darrow

Exhausted from walking up the stairs of the earl's manor, Josi followed the butler into the room. The gilded frames and crimson walls were indicative of a higher status. Wealth and circumstance surrounded her with dark paneling and ornate molding. Even the ceiling held carved cherubs in the corners.

"I'll be back with your trunk, my lady." Brenner disappeared. Days before, he'd insisted on retrieving her few belongings from her home. She'd wanted to return home, but with her mare being found and stabled here at the earl's, Josi had stayed. And now, both Lord Fennyson and his butler had somehow convinced Josi to stay in a guest room. She'd hoped to be on the mend and on her way by now.

With a heavy sigh, she sat on the bed, crimson curtains adorning each post. A muffled voice came through the walls to her right. A door was in the center of the wall—with an adjacent door to another room. Josi was in *the* room—the countess's room attached to Lord Fennyson's. She slunk back against the pillows. Her late husband must be rolling in his grave. Lady Greyen would be in a fit when she found out.

The earl had intercepted Lady Greyen every morning for the past week, refusing to allow her past the entryway. Her shrill voice would carry into the study—until today, when Lord Fennyson ordered Brenner to guide Josi upstairs, instructing Brenner to help her. Josi had hoped to go home and speak with her sweet housekeeper. But she tired too quickly.

There was another worry. If her dizziness persisted, she wouldn't be able to travel back to California.

Footsteps echoed from the corridor. Brenner emerged with her trunk in tow and tucked it in the corner. He turned to leave and glanced at her. "You seem unsure, Lady Darrow."

"This is the countess's room, isn't it?" Not even in her own home did Josi live in the mistress quarters. That room was reserved for Lady Greyen's frequent visits—Josi's husband put his mother above his wife. The baroness lived in the next county over but seemed to appear whenever Josi became brave enough to move her things into the room. The simple stable was a safer area, a place Lady Greyen avoided. The baroness would never forgive Josi's mare for her son's death. Nor would she welcome Josi into the family as anything more than a temporary distraction.

"Lady Darrow, are you uncomfortable with this room?" Brenner's voice was smooth, Josi guessed, from many years soothing the temperamental earl. His cadence and tone did have a calming effect.

"It feels improper." Josi might have fallen, but she did live next door. If Lady Greyen wasn't lurking about, Josi could have easily recovered, until she heard back from her father. "Lord Fennyson isn't married." *And neither am I.*

Holding up a finger, Brenner walked to the door connecting the master and mistress rooms. Twisting the knob, he made a show of the door being locked. "I can assure you, your character is safe."

"I doubt Lady Greyen will agree," she murmured. The baroness had a way of sniffing out information regarding Josi.

Lord Fennyson burst through the door, his enormous frame filling the room. "What happened?"

Both Brenner and Josi exchanged a look of surprise.

"I heard rattling." Lord Fennyson's gaze found Josi—concern in his eye. The worry melted Josi's hesitation. Mr. Thatcher's words echoed in her mind, *Lord Fennyson will always protect his friends.* Safe. Josi could recover in peace if she stayed in Lord Fennyson's home rather than her own. The thought washed over her.

Brenner grinned. "Lady Darrow was worried about the improper nature of your rooms sharing a door."

"The door locks from this side." With long strides, the earl checked the knob, then paused, his back stiffening. "You …" He turned slowly, his expression unreadable. "You were scared of me coming through the door?"

Brenner's eyes widened. He discreetly slipped from the room, leaving Josi alone with the earl—improper yet again. She started to speak. "Lady Greyen—"

"Is nothing but a church bell that shouldn't be rung." Lord Fennyson began pacing, a hand on his face, the other on his hip. "That family is a miserable lot." He paused. "Be careful, Lady Darrow. I'd rather tempt my fate with the wolves out there than with the baroness. She'd stab you, then curse you for dirtying her knife."

Josi hung her head in her hands. There was a secret she'd not dared to tell her father. One she worried Lady Greyen knew. "She doesn't need to stab me, she only needs a confession."

"You can't be faulted for your husband's death." He kneeled in front of her, his shoulders wide. "And you needn't worry about Freya. She has a home here, no matter what the baroness says."

"Thank you." His offer should have taken the weight off Josi's shoulders. But there was little relief. She was trying desperately to keep a roof over her head and the wolves at bay.

"Was he kind to you?"

"I do not think kindness is anywhere in that family's pedigree. But no, he never took a hand against me."

Lord Fennyson reached for her, threading their fingers together. A curious hum crept up her arm. His thumb made gentle circles on her skin. "My father had a way of making my mother feel small." His eyes widened as if he was shocked by his admission.

She squeezed his hand, warmth spreading over her. "My father had a way of making me feel seen."

"That must be a sight to behold." His eyes crinkled, the flecks of gold winking at her. He scooted closer, and his eyes widened again, appearing surprised at his actions.

His shock gave her confidence. She wondered if his heart hammered away in his chest like hers. His lips turned up in a crooked grin. She felt the warmth of a blush.

"Or perhaps this is a better sight." Lord Fennyson chuckled as she felt her face turn hotter still.

Slipping her hand from his, she covered her face. "I cannot help it."

"It's a delight." He pulled her hands down, his face inches from her. "I didn't know teasing an *argylwyddes* would be so diverting."

Her pulse pounded as his breath tickled her lips. She opened her mouth to speak, but her mind went blank. She'd not been here before. He came closer, their lips nearly touching.

Words. She needed words out of her mouth. "Lord …" By jove, she'd forgotten his name.

"Cyril."

"Cyril." Grinning like a schoolgirl, a chuckle escaped. She should not be addressing him so informally. "We have fully ventured into improper waters."

"I aim to please." He lifted her hand and pressed it against his patched cheek.

Her heart skipped a beat, and her palms began sweating. She needed to say something, anything. "I'm not a good wife."

Retreating, Cyril raised his eyebrows. "Was that Sir John's opinion?"

A draft between them cooled Josi's pulse. Cyril had a right to know. His perspective of Lady Darrow's character was about to change. "We were married in name only."

"In name only …" Cyril spoke slowly, a questioning lilt to each word.

Her head back in her hands, Josi groaned. "Lady Greyen knows.

Sir John must have told her. He was looking for a legal loophole. A way to annul the marriage for another wife."

"Another wife."

"He spent the dowry and needed more money."

Lord Fennyson coughed into his fist. "A man cannot dispose of a wife after he's wrung her dry."

"If the marriage was never …" Her face must be blindingly red, her embarrassment palpable. "If the marriage was in name only, then Sir John could claim I wasn't dutiful and be granted an annulment."

He arched an eyebrow. "I'm not a solicitor, but that cannot be legal."

Josi swallowed the rising emotion. She'd thought Cyril—a Welsh gentleman—would criticize her, call her out for failing as a woman. Perhaps not all Welsh men thought of women as little more than property. "He died before anything could be done."

"Do you know who is next in line?" Cyril's voice was a caress over her.

"No idea. I just know the vultures are circling." And the wolves. "I have a year of mourning." She glanced down at her dress, the fashion out of date and far too creamy for her liking. In the States, she wore riding habits from sunrise to sunset. Tea parties were for the American grandmothers eager to gossip about their grandchildren's antics. "But in truth, I've even less time. I'd hope to sell off his shepherds, or at least use them to guard the property. The wolves have preyed on nearly all I have left."

He sat next to her on the bed, the mattress shifting under his weight. "The wolves are coming dangerously close." He rubbed the back of his neck. "It's not natural, and their numbers are growing. But stealing shepherds, that doesn't make much sense."

"I thought some of the prints were from Sir John's dogs, but only a person could open each kennel door. Not a wolf."

"I meant what I said." Playfully, he elbowed her. The moment gave her strength. "Freya has a home here. As do you."

She swallowed the rising emotion. Her father was just as generous, a weakness in Sir John's eyes. A burst of protectiveness came over her. "Be careful, Lord Fennyson—"

"Cyril."

"Be careful, Cyril. Lady Greyen will use your kindness as a weapon." She hugged herself. She'd imagined her marriage to be like this, an easy flow between two people. "I wrote to my father. He set aside earnings from the racehorses I helped with. He didn't want to send over the earnings until I felt at home here."

"If he sent those earnings—"

"They would have been the property of Sir John." She risked a glance at him. She was oblivious to the patched skin or scars littering his face; she saw only concern and worry. "I asked him for a portion. But not to stay here, for passage to return home."

He ran his hands down his face. "You're leaving."

"I know I'm a coward for tucking tail and returning home. But here, I'm friendless. Lonely."

He pulled her to a stand and lifted her hand to his lips. "You're not friendless."

CHAPTER 10

*C*yril Heathclove, Lord Fennyson

With an arm around her, Cyril helped Lady Darrow—*Josi*—from the dining room out to his stables. She was able to keep some broth down but little else.

The manor was still firmly in the Edwardian era of his grandfather, but Cyril had spared no expense on modernizing the home for his herd. Pride danced along his skin as he watched Josi fawn over the details of each stall, complete with modern plumbing.

"Ah, Freya." Josi cooed to her mare, unlatching the stall door. She ran a hand down the horse's front leg, eying the stitches Cyril had sewn. "What happened?"

"She's a horse. It could have been anything. The blasted creatures could find a needle in the hay mound, slicing themselves from side to side." Like flies to pigsties, injuries flocked to horses. Heaven knows, Cyril spent hours tending to the beasts and all their creative ways they could hurt themselves.

Her hands ran along the withers, spine, and down the back legs. Freya nickered at the attention. "I don't think she came in contact with the wolves." Josi came back to Freya's neck. Turning around, she leaned her back against the horse's shoulder. The mare searched Josi's hands for treats, its velvet nose twitching eagerly. Sighing, Josi closed her eyes briefly.

"Dizzy?" Cyril was at her side in an instant.

She peered up him, a question in her eyes. Her coloring was still off, but she moved with less effort, her gait steadier.

"It gets easier." He held out his arm.

She tilted her head, reminding Cyril of Beowulf. "This isn't my first fall."

"Nor mine." He wrapped an arm around her back and waited for her to take the first step.

Her breathing grew shallower. She'd done too much today. Perhaps moving her to an upstairs room was an ill-advised attempt to give her more rest. He felt calmer having their rooms connected. Even with her ability to lock the door, having Josi just a few feet away took a weight off his shoulder.

Josi's short marriage was a puzzle—one Josi was clearly embarrassed by. Cyril's parents were happy, once. He'd heard of them being in love, but his illness had flared his father's drinking habits. His skin had driven a wedge between them.

Josi had been married mere months. Their love should have been shiny and new, not cold and lonely—if Sir John was capable of affection at all.

Out of the stables, Josi stopped and let her head fall back. "I miss this."

Glancing around, Cyril looked for what she meant. They stood between the house and the stable, nothing unusual.

"Why must it rain so often?" Opening her eyes, Josi lowered her chin.

"You miss the sun?"

She stepped to the side and held out her arms. "Tell me that doesn't feel wonderful. Convince me the warmth doesn't fill your soul."

"You've gone mad." Cyril watched as she tried to spin in a slow circle. "Careful, Josi."

Her cheeks blushed at *Josi*. "Thank you for your kindness."

"Are you truly miserable?" Two long strides and Cyril was at her side.

Josi swallowed hard, her smile hesitant. "It's been less lonely of late."

He took in the sight of her. Her black hair was in a simple plait, loose strands framing her face. Her icy blue eyes were lit with joy. He stepped closer, her cheeks blushing adorably. There was an innocence about her, pulling him in and drawing him close. For most of his life, Cyril had been prickly to those who dared come near. He'd been lonely. Miserable.

"Stay," he whispered. "I can't stop the rain, and I can't promise the sun, but stay, Josi."

Her delicate lips parted. Her eyes widened. "Stay?"

"I don't have the charm of Sir John." Hesitating, he pointed to his face. "I'll never have the look of a distinguished earl, but let me prove the honor of a true Welsh gentleman."

Josi pulled his hand away from his face. "I like your scars." She shrugged. "Reminds me of home, in a way. I was of more use on the ranch. I could stitch. I could ride. I could fix things."

I like your scars. His pulse raced, hammering in his chest. His tongue was thick, awkward. Speaking shouldn't be this difficult. "Lady Greyen has given you a year, yes?"

"According to the solicitor, the family must return the dowry once my mourning season is over." With a slight shake of her head, Josi smiled sadly. "For all their pomp and circumstance, I do not believe they have the money. The property is entailed and can't be liquidated, only inherited." She sighed, the sorrow in her blue eyes tugging at his heart. "And so I wrote to my father, Cyril."

His name on her lips sent a thrill up his spine. He'd lost his mind. "Stay." His hand in hers, he pulled her close. "Freya will be taken care of here. I know we're strangers, Josi, and I'm not the type of man to make a woman swoon—"

"Swoon?" Josi covered her mouth, her eyes crinkling.

"I can't find the right words." He was making a fool of himself. For once, he needed to be a master of his tongue. "I just want you to stay."

Her hand fell to her side.

He swallowed against the rising panic, words tumbling from him "I feel like a gentleman, a seen person, when you're around."

Her mouth formed an O.

Blast it all. He was rambling like a fool. The words kept coming. "You don't flinch or stare at my face. I've not talked to anyone the way I talk with you."

The beginnings of a smile appeared, giving him hope.

He nervously tugged on the end of her plait. "Brenner is good and kind, but he's not near as fair as you, *argylwyddes.*"

Her gaze flicked to the ground, to his shoulders, everywhere but his eyes. "Would you be angry if I don't know my mind yet?"

The evening air added a layer of intimacy. He stepped closer, the temptation to hold her hand grew.

She murmured, "I thought I'd learned my lesson." Her smiled faltered "Trusting a... stranger..." her voice went high at *stranger.* "Trusting a stranger shouldn't be so easy."

"I'd be satisfied knowing you're considering the option." Time was all he needed. Hiding away in his manor, Cyril had spent most of his life ashamed of his face. Here was an *argylwyddes* who didn't give a fig about his appearance. She'd been hurt by a fellow gentleman, and he couldn't blame her. Cyril could prove his devotion, given enough time.

"I'm considering." Her cheeks were ablaze once more.

Cupping her chin, he tilted her face upward. She inhaled sharply as he brushed his thumb across her lips.

"I believe I've found the true wolf," Lady Greyen snapped.

Josi recoiled. Cyril jumped back, a slew of curses falling from his lips.

"How am I not to be suspicious of your intentions, Lord Fennyson?" The baroness narrowed her eyes at them, her voice shrill.

Brenner came up beside the baroness, an apology in his eyes. "Her ladyship was very insistent."

"You are damaging my son's good name." Lady Greyen clenched

her fists at her side, reminding Cyril of a toddler. Her nostrils flared. He waited for her to paw at the ground like a bull and charge at them.

"Your son never possessed a good name." Cyril couldn't help disparaging the horrible man. It was ill-tempered to speak of the dead, but he felt a surge of protectiveness over Josi. He'd never felt this way before. Pulling on his cravat, Cyril wondered if he was any better than Sir John. He knew Josi was in a predicament and needed assistance but doubted she wanted this type of help. She'd resented his offering at the ridge several days before. Cyril wanted happiness for her—even if that meant leaving for the States.

"You are a spoiled, naïve child." Lady Greyen pointed a trembling finger at Josi. "I've been generous—"

"No," Josi said quietly, her hands wringing. "You've been cruel, never kind."

"How dare—"

"I'm sorry about Sir John." Josi's voice wavered. "I warned him not to ride Freya, but he wouldn't—"

"Put that horse down!" Lady Greyen screamed, her hands over her ears as she cried out. "You don't even have the decency to mourn my son."

Groaning, Cyril pointed at Lady Greyen. Josi put a hand on his arm. She blinked back moisture and left his side. Softly, she pulled the baroness by the arm toward the house. He wanted to hurl insults at the shrewd lady but found himself following behind Josi.

In the living room, Lady Greyen paced while Josi braced herself against the sofa. Cyril came to her and said softly, "You need to rest, Josi." When she didn't budge, Cyril added, "Brenner will send for Lady Greyen's footmen. I'll help you upstairs."

CHAPTER 11

*L*ady Josephine Darrow

With Lady Greyen in the study below, and Cyril at Josi's side, assisting with each step on the stairs, Josi felt both guilt and a heavy dose of giddiness. Sir John had never reached for her hand. He'd spill pretty words on paper but not once from his lips. After he passed, Josi reread the letters they'd exchanged. The man she'd fallen in love with only existed in empty words. Sir John in the flesh was distant and withdrawn. He was more interested in proving his superiority to his family, his neighbors—everyone but his own wife.

And yet, the giant of a man with his arm supporting her was supposed to be the brute. Villagers whispered about him. If he strode into town, others would cross the street and avoid eye contact. With each passing moment, Cyril reminded her more of her father. Tall, quiet—and kind.

The temptation to stay was growing, but she'd been deceived before. Cyril had never written her. She only knew what she experienced so far—a direct contradiction to her courtship with Sir John.

"I can't stay here." Josi turned at the top step, a hand on the rail.

The sun dipped below the horizon, taking the last of the warm day with it.

"I won't bully you into staying in Wales." He descended a step, her head now at his shoulders.

Josi waved an arm over the rail. "I meant here. At your home."

"Oh." His mouth formed an O. Another step down.

"It is beyond improper." She felt darker at the thought of leaving. Heathclove Manor had been more of a home than the roof she shared with Sir John. "If there is to be a future between us, our union would be plagued with impropriety."

Without meeting her gaze, he nodded. "I understand."

"That is more than I can say. I don't understand. I don't know how to begin to understand." Josi ran a finger along the wooden rail. "I cannot account for how I feel. I don't understand this—I don't understand *us*." By jove, she'd gone mad. *Us?* She felt her cheeks warm. There couldn't be an *us* just as she couldn't be in Wales any longer. Cyril was just as much of a stranger as Sir John was—a lump formed in her throat. She'd felt more at ease in Cyril's presence than she'd ever felt with her husband. Sir John had never stood up for her or demanded that the baroness leave her be. Even now, with her head and body worn out, she felt stronger with Cyril near.

"Perhaps..." In one big stride, Cyril cleared both steps. "We can venture into foreign territories together."

"Together?" Her voice cracked. She felt her face flush deeper still.

He winked at her and guided her into the room. Helping her sit on the bed, he added, "For the record, I don't give a fig about a dowry. Or a mourning period."

"Oh." She swallowed hard, the room suddenly warm despite the evening air.

Brenner burst into the room, his brow furrowed in worry. "I've called for Thatcher for the baroness, but I'm afraid the good doctor is gone. He was only in town for a few days."

"A doctor?" There was no need for a doctor, but both Cyril and Brenner exchanged a knowing glance. Something was amiss. "You're distressed over her not seeing a physician? She's angry, not injured."

"A tonic, Lady Darrow." Brenner frowned, hesitation in his words. "I readied her carriage and sent for a doctor. When I returned to the reception room, she was gone."

"Gone?" Josi gasped. "She's after Freya." Lady Greyen had threatened many times before.

Pity crossed Brenner's features. He added quietly, "I've sent for some men."

"Blasted woman," Cyril thundered.

"She'll kill Freya." Josi couldn't let that happen.

"Stay here. You can't help and should be resting." Without another word, Cyril bounded from the room, Brenner on his heels.

With achingly slow steps, Josi shuffled down the stairs and out to the moonlit stables. Her horse and four other horses seemed to be missing. Freya would not be used; Cyril would have kept the mare in the stall. A chill swept across Josi's neck as Lady Greyen's threats echoed in her mind. The baroness hated Freya with every ounce of venom she possessed. Josi walked down the long line of mares and geldings to the stallion stable, praying Cyril had left his stallion home. Speed was needed to chase after Lady Greyen, leaving the heavy Percherons. Josi needed steady not a neck-breaking pace.

Atlas called out, his neigh echoing into the night air. Quick as she could, Josi found the nearest bridle and slipped it over the stallion's head. The horse was massive. She opened the stall door but spun Atlas around, facing him toward the back of the stall. Climbing up the edge of the stall, she grabbed fistfuls of mane and launched herself on him. The world spun. She inhaled sharply and waited for the dizziness to pass. Her stomach twisted. Perhaps Cyril was right. She should be resting. But she knew Lady Greyen's mind. Long before the baroness was a grieving mother, she would obsess over an idea until she'd run over every obstacle—Josi included.

Gently, she squeezed her legs, praying the stallion would move slowly. It stepped forward a few paces, its neck arched. A neigh rippled through its chest. Leaning forward, Josi relaxed her legs. The last thing she needed was to accidentally cue Atlas into a gallop.

A horse called out. Atlas tensed. *Relax*, Josi commanded. She would not be able to hold on if Atlas decided to take off. Guiding the stallion to the ridge, she focused on breathing slowly. Steadily. A wolf howled in the distance. She winced as a growl just below answered.

Under the light of the moon, Josi saw the star on Beowulf's forehead. The shepherd had followed her. "Bless you, Beowulf."

There was movement up ahead, near her home. *Wolves.* The pack would steal the last of her chickens. A trail of lanterns made their way up toward Heathclove Manor. Brenner must have alerted the villagers, but she doubted they knew of the wolves. She hadn't been able to get them to respond to simple small talk, let alone a conversation about predators.

Josi urged Atlas forward, his long legs covering the ground. Closer still, the outline of a person became visible under the dim moonlight. *Not a wolf.* A chill ran down her spine. Josi saw the bell shape of a skirt. A woman was leaving the chicken coop, a bag on her arm. Beowulf growled at Josi's feet. The muffled sounds of sleepy chickens echoed in the quiet night.

With the bag over her shoulder, the woman snuck over to the pigsty, kicking at the fence. And then another woman followed after her. Grunting, the first woman set the bag down, and the moon revealed her face—Lady Greyen.

Shock turned to frustration. A fist in the mane, Josi shouted, "Stop."

The second woman cowered. Under the moonlight, Josi saw her sweet housekeeper. Josi gripped the mane and felt every inch of the servant's betrayal.

"I'm sorry, milady." The housekeeper scurried off.

"Get back here!" Lady Greyen called after the servant before facing Josi. "Get off my land."

"Lady Greyen." Josi could barely say the words. She wanted nothing more than to run after her friend. Memories rushed through her. Twice, Josi had misread someone, thinking she had an ally. First her husband and now her housekeeper. Josi squeezed her legs, urging Atlas forward. *"You're* the wolf. You stole the dogs. The chickens. It's been you this entire time."

"How dare you?" The baroness spat on the ground. "How dare you, *you* a simple harlot—how dare you accuse me of stealing my own animals from my own land." Beowulf growled and began circling Lady Greyen. Pulling a chicken from the bag, she tossed the animal toward the dog. Beowulf wasn't distracted, keeping its focus on the baroness. "You've destroyed my family. Killed my son. And now, you keep company with the earl. *Lord Fennyson.* The family that stole—"

"Your son spent the dowry before I stepped foot on this land. The earl has been nothing but—"

"Do not lie to me." The baroness tossed another chicken. It squawked and flapped. Atlas tensed, ears flicking—body tense. "Your dowry helped feed your own stomach." She shook a chicken, clutching it by its feet. "The chickens. The pigs. All of that was for you." Lady Greyen scowled. "Ask me, Josephine. Ask me why there were no animals on our land."

"Lady—"

"Ask me!" She ran up to Josi.

Atlas shied. Gripping the stallion with everything she had, Josi tried to keep her seat. Her stomach twisted. Beowulf snapped at the baroness, making Atlas hop to the side. Josi's stomach lurched. She slipped from Atlas's back—sighing when her boots found the ground. Atlas danced next to Josi, unsure of what or where to go.

"They bred wolves, Josephine. They bred these beasts." Lady Greyen shouted at the shepherd circling her, its teeth bared. Stumbling back, Josi's boot caught, and she fell to the ground. The baroness leered over Josi. "They devoured our livestock. Everything. And now you've—"

"Stop!" Josi shouted. Whimpering, Beowulf sniffed her face and licked her hand. "The feud between families is none of my concern. You were cruel to me. Your son was—"

"Do not—"

"Cyril was kind. You would have left me on the ridge, my head injured. You would have felt relief at not paying the dowry back. Cyril didn't owe me anything. He didn't have to help me—"

Lady Greyen launched herself at Josi. Beowulf snapped, teeth digging into the skirt of the baroness. The sound of movement grew behind Josi. She turned. Several villagers held up lanterns, their faces in different stages of surprise.

"Shoot this animal!" the baroness screamed.

"Lady Greyen," a masculine voice called out. *Cyril.* Relief washed over Josi. The villagers parted, allowing Cyril to come forward, leading Freya. "Beowulf."

The shepherd obediently released the baroness, returning to a tight circle. Cyril held out an arm, indicating the baroness. "I fear I owe the village an apology."

Lady Greyen spat at the ground.

"It appears a wolf was in our midst." Cyril came to Josi's side. "I believe I'm in need of a solicitor. Lady Greyen, we will have our day in court." Ignoring her screams, Cyril gave the baroness his back and helped Josi to her feet. "Ah, *argylwyddes,* do you ever listen?"

Warmth pulsed in her veins. He scooped Josi up and cradled her against his chest.

She wrapped her arms around him, clinging to his frame. "My father … he taught me to stitch an injury and get back on a horse when I fell. I couldn't let my horse…" she sniffed.

"Your father would be proud." His voice caressed her. "Not every lady would charge into the night after her horse."

She lifted her head. "You're not angry?"

"Oh, *argylwyddes,* don't misunderstand me. Your attic is for rent, that is true. It wouldn't hurt for you to rest instead of barreling ahead —but no, I'm not angry." He carefully placed her on Atlas and then swung up behind her. "Although you did steal my horse. That's a hanging offense."

Instead of answering, she leaned against his chest, bringing his arms around her.

He kissed her neck and sent shivers down her spine. "Hone. Let's go home, Josi."

EPILOGUE

$\mathcal{C}$yril Heathclove, Lord Fennyson

The dark-haired minx with blue eyes would be the death of Cyril. At only five years old, Esther had wrapped her tiny hands around Cyril's heart. He winced, watching her ride Freya. She refused to learn on his old stallion, opting for the more spirited mare.

Josi looped her arm through his, whispering, "Breathe, Cyril."

"She should be riding a rocking horse. A wooden one that won't buck her off." He growled, then cursed.

"Easy, boy," Josi teased and rubbed her growing belly. She'd hoped for a boy, but Cyril wanted another girl.

He pulled Josi close, wrapping his arms around her. She laid her head on his chest, pouring comfort into his being. This was why Wales needed another set of icy blue eyes. They had a way of spreading warmth and sunshine. Her father had visited once a year, every summer. He'd been hesitant at first but somehow, someway, Cyril had convinced the father of his love for Josi. A kind man, Cyril desperately hoped his gentle father-in-law's genes would take over if a boy arrived.

Esther squealed with delight when Freya shifted from canter to trot. Cyril cursed while Josi chuckled.

Threading her fingers through his, Josi whispered, "Brenner hasn't let go of the lead rope. Freya can only go so far."

"I don't know who I trust least, Brenner or Freya," Cyril grumbled. "She's not even scared."

"She's too innocent to be frightened." Josi stepped back. "I suppose that's my fault. It could have saved me a lot of heartache if I was less naïve."

Pulling her back into his arms, he cupped her chin. "Oh, but your heart is what captured mine, *argylwyddes.* I think loving is the bravest thing we can do."

Her lips stretched to a wide grin. "What if part of that love is reserved for horses, particularly spirited little mares?"

"That mare is not little."

Josi wrapped her arms around his neck. "Neither are you."

He leaned in and brushed his lips against hers. "I suppose I should be grateful for Freya. She did throw you in my arms, so to speak."

Smiling against his lips, Josi whispered, "Don't speak."

ALSO BY CLARISSA KAE

Once Upon a Fairy Tale

(Multi author anthology)

Time Slip Novels

Of Ink And Sea

Women's Fiction

Pieces To Mend

Once And Future Wife Series

Once And Future Wife

Disorder in the Veins (2023)

Scarlet Pimpernel Victorian Spy Series

A Sapphire Sphinx

Victorian Retellings

A Dark Beauty, Beauty & the Beast

Cinders Like Glass , Cinderella

A Stolen Heart, Robin Hood

Taming Christmas, Taming of the Shrew (standalone)

ABOUT THE AUTHOR

Clarissa Kae is a preeminent voice whose professional career began as a freelance editor in 2007. She's the former president of her local California Writers Club after spending several years as the Critique Director.

Since her first novel, she's explored different writing genres and created a loyal group of fans who eagerly await her upcoming release. With numerous awards to her name, Clarissa continues to honor the role of storyteller.

Aside from the writing community, she and her daughters founded Kind Girls Make Strong Women to help undervalued nonprofit organizations—from reuniting children with families to giving Junior Olympic athletes their shot at success.

She lives in the agricultural belly of California with her family and farm of horses, chickens, dogs and kittens aplenty.

www.clarissakae.com